DEEG AND DOOF GO TO THE ZOO

Om KIDZ
An imprint of Om Books International

Om KIDZ | Om Books International

Reprinted in 2025

Corporate & Editorial Office
A-12, Sector 64, Noida 201 301
Uttar Pradesh, India
Phone: +91 120 477 4100
Email: editorial@ombooks.com
Website: www.ombooksinternational.com

Sales Office
107, Ansari Road, Darya Ganj
New Delhi 110 002, India
Phone: +91 11 4000 9000
Email: sales@ombooks.com
Website: www.ombooks.com

ISBN: 978-93-85273-84-1

Printed in India

10 9 8 7 6 5

DEEG AND DOOF GO TO THE ZOO

I'm all set to read

Paste your photograph here

My name is

Deeg and **Doof** are **aliens** from outer **space.** They have come to Earth to **make new** friends. Once they are on Earth, they wonder where to go.

"Where can we **find** different **kinds** of Earthlings in one **place**?" asks **Deeg**. This gives **Doof** an **idea**. He **excitedly** tells **Deeg** his **idea**.

"Let's go to the **zoo**," says **Doof.** "It is not **too** far from here." "There are many different **kinds** of Earthlings there," he explains.

So, **Deeg** and **Doof** go to the **zoo**. When they **reach** there, they are very happy to see so many different **types** of animals.

ZOO

Deeg and **Doof** want to **make** friends with all the animals in the **zoo.** They want to **meet** and talk to everyone.

But the animals in the **zoo** are very afraid of **Deeg** and **Doof**. **Deeg** and **Doof** don't look **like** anyone the animals have ever met.

Deeg and **Doof** are different! None of the creatures on Earth have such strange colours. All the animals become wary of **Deeg** and **Doof.**

Deeg and **Doof** go to **meet** the **kangaroo**. The **kangaroo** gets scared and backs **away**. **Deeg** and **Doof** **feel** sad, but they move on.

Next, **Deeg** and **Doof** go to **meet** the **cheetah**. The **cheetah** looks at the **aliens** and starts growling angrily.

Deeg and **Doof** don't want to upset anyone, so they **resume** walking.

Soon, they come across the **snake** family. Mrs **Snake** doesn't want the **aliens speaking** with her children. She hisses at **Deeg** and **Doof** to go **away**.

Poor Deeg and **Doof**!
Nobody wants to talk to them.

Nobody wants to be with them.
What can **they** both do to **make** friends on Earth?

All of a sudden, **Deeg** gets an **idea.** He whispers his plan in **Doof's** ear. They both stand in front of all the animals and start singing.

“We come here from outer **space**
with a different body and **face**.
Let us start some happy trends
and begin by being good friends!”

All the animals in the **zoo** like the song. They start singing and dancing along. And that is how **Deeg** and **Doof finally make** friends with Earthlings.

Know your phonic words

These words have the long "a" , "e", "i", "oo" and "u" sounds in them.

"a"

aliens
space
make
place
away
face
snake
they

"e"

Deeg
reach
meet
cheetah
feel
speaking
reach

"i'

find
kinds
idea
excitedly
types
like
finally

"oo"

Doof
zoo
too
kangaroo
soon
poor

"u"

new
resume